FAVOURITE Fairy STORIES

An illustrated treasury

FAVOURITE Fairy STORIES

An illustrated treasury

LITTLE TIGER

LONDON

Contents

The Snow Fairy

Written by Lucy M. George

Illustrated by Rosie Butcher

The Snow Fairy

Isabel woke up early one morning. Something was different, she could feel it in the air. She opened the curtains wide and gasped at the sight. "Wow," she whispered in awe. "Snow!"

For as far as she could see, thick snow coated the ground. It was piled on the trees and heaped on the hills. Tiny flakes shone in the sky, and everything glistened.

"Can we play in the snow?" Isabel asked, running to the kitchen where her parents were making breakfast.

"Of course!" said her mother. "We should build a snowman!"

After breakfast, her father helped her put on cosy gloves and a woolly hat and she ran out into the wintery wonderland of the garden.

The snow crunched under her feet. "Come on!" cried Isabel impatiently. As they gathered up piles of snow for their snowman, her parents told her a story.

"Do you know the one about the snow fairies?" her father asked, patting the snowman's round tummy. "People say that they help lost travellers find their way home."

"What do they look like?" asked Isabel, scooping up some snow for the snowman's feet.

"No one knows," said her mother, giving the snowman two branches for arms. "No one has ever seen a snow fairy."

"Then how can people believe in them?"

"There are lots of things we can't see that are real," said her father. "And they say that when a snow fairy helps you, they give you a magical snowflake, which never melts, to remind you to be careful in the snow."

"I want to see a snow fairy!" said Isabel. Her parents lifted her up and she gave the snowman button eyes, a carrot for a nose and a big smile.

"He looks wonderful!" said her mother. "We'd better go in now though, it's nearly lunchtime."

"But I want to see a snow fairy!" said Isabel. "Can I stay and look for one?"

"Okay," said her father, "just for a few minutes, and make sure you stay in the garden."

"I will, I promise!"

Isabel looked around the garden, searching high and low, but she couldn't find a snow fairy anywhere. Her heart sank. "I suppose I'll never see one!" she said, sitting down in the thick snow beside the snowman.

But just then, she saw a flutter in the trees at the end of the garden by the stream. She leapt up and ran towards it. Could it be a snow fairy? She hurried through the trees, but there was nothing to be seen.

Then a glimmer of light caught her eye across the stream. Maybe this was a snow fairy? She raced into the snowy meadow, and across the frosty grass she saw a tiny silhouette. Her eyes sparkling, Isabel ran up the hill, chasing the little shape. It had to be a snow fairy! She reached the top, her heart beating fast . . . But there was nothing there. Where had the fairy gone?

Isabel's heart sank. She had so longed to see a snow fairy. Maybe they didn't exist after all.

Then she looked up and realised she had left the garden, and her home, far behind her. A cold wind blew and dark snow clouds gathered in the gloomy sky. Suddenly it began to snow. Flakes fell so thick and fast that Isabel couldn't even see her feet.

She stood in the icy mist and shivered. Hot tears rolled over her frozen cheeks. She was lost! "How will I ever find my way home?" she cried. Her parents would be so worried!

Just then Isabel thought she heard a fluttering beside her. She peered into the whiteness all around her, but all she could see was snow. Then she felt a tiny tug at her sleeve, so gentle she wasn't quite sure whether she had imagined it.

There it was again! Was it a snow fairy at last? It pulled lightly, and she followed. She was cold and with every step she longed for home.

The snow was slowing now, and at last she could hear her parents' voices calling for her. "I'm here! I'm coming!" she called back.

She stumbled into the garden, where she saw her mother and father searching for her. Just then the tug at Isabel's sleeve fell away, and the fluttering sound grew fainter and disappeared. Isabel and her parents rushed towards each other.

"Hush," said her father, scooping Isabel into his arms and carrying her into the warm house. "You're safe now."

18

"Where have you been?" said her mother, sitting her beside the fire. "We've been looking for you everywhere!"

"I'm sorry," Isabel cried, holding her parents close. "I was looking for a snow fairy and I got lost! I'll never wander off alone again."

"So, did you find your snow fairy?" asked her mother.

Isabel looked out into the garden. There was nothing but snow and the snowman. But then she opened her hand . . . And there, lying on her warm mitten, beside the roaring fire, was a perfect snowflake.

"No," she said, staring at the unmelting snowflake. "No one's ever seen a snow fairy. But I do believe in them."

20

The Midsummer Boat Race

Written by Emily Hibbs

Illustrated by Rachel Baines

The Midsummer Boat Race

"Perfect!" Kiara declared, peering closely at the tiny shells in her palm. She looked over at the little boat tied up to her garden fence and smiled proudly. It had taken her weeks to build – from hours spent looking for the best birch tree branch for the silver mast, to searching high and low for the shiniest leaf sail, everything had been planned to the smallest detail.

Kiara skipped over to the garden fence, her pockets jangling with all the shells she'd collected ready to decorate her boat. They would be the perfect finishing touch! Kiara couldn't wait for the Midsummer Boat Race tomorrow.

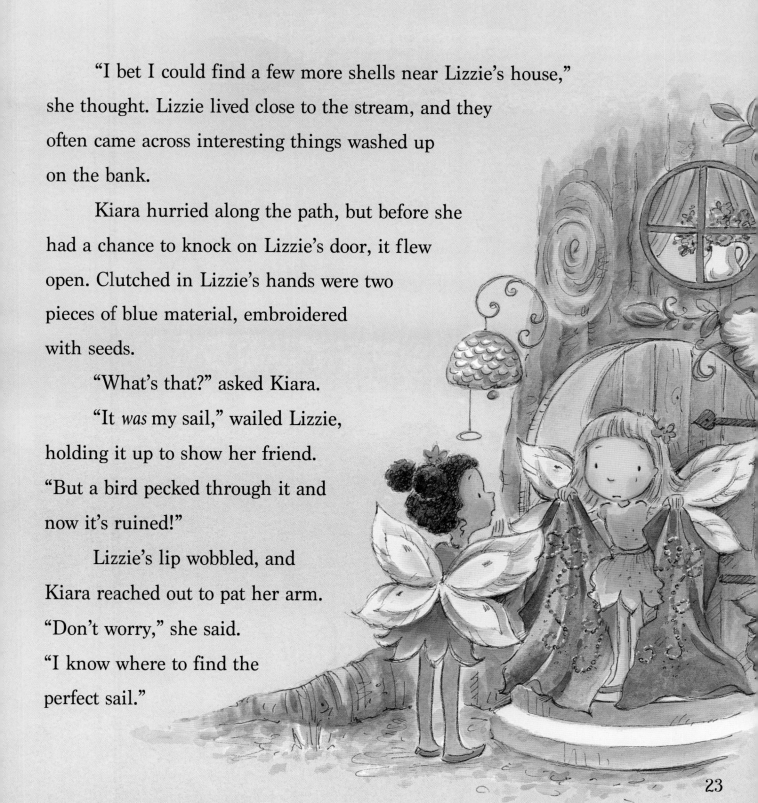

"I bet I could find a few more shells near Lizzie's house," she thought. Lizzie lived close to the stream, and they often came across interesting things washed up on the bank.

Kiara hurried along the path, but before she had a chance to knock on Lizzie's door, it flew open. Clutched in Lizzie's hands were two pieces of blue material, embroidered with seeds.

"What's that?" asked Kiara.

"It *was* my sail," wailed Lizzie, holding it up to show her friend. "But a bird pecked through it and now it's ruined!"

Lizzie's lip wobbled, and Kiara reached out to pat her arm. "Don't worry," she said. "I know where to find the perfect sail."

23

Kiara flew quickly back to her house and untied the leaf sail from her boat. "I've got lots of time to find a new one," she told herself. "And Lizzie will be really upset if she can't race tomorrow – she's been looking forward to it so much!"

Lizzie was delighted with the sail; she held it in her arms and twirled around in excitement. "Thank you, Kiara!" she cried. They tied it on to Lizzie's boat, then Kiara set off to find a replacement.

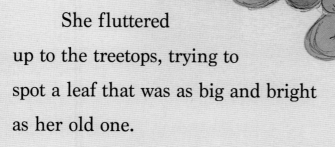

She fluttered
up to the treetops, trying to
spot a leaf that was as big and bright
as her old one.

"Woah!" A voice nearby made her jump.
Kiara spun around to see her friend Jack
tugging on a loose branch in a neighbouring
tree. He lost his grip and tumbled backwards!
Fluttering her wings, Kiara darted towards
him and caught his hand. Together,
they flew to the ground.

"Thanks, Kiara!" said Jack.

"What were you doing?" Kiara
asked, alarmed.

"I was trying to reach that branch
to use as a mast for my boat," Jack said,
pointing up at it. "I *had* a brilliant mast,
but then I left my boat outside in a windy
spot and the mast snapped."

Jack stared glumly at the tree, his wings drooping. The branch he'd been trying to reach was quite wonky – not really the best sort of shape for a mast.

Kiara thought for a moment. "I know where we can find the perfect mast," she called, as she whirled up into the air and flew towards home.

When Kiara returned with her silver birch tree branch, a huge smile spread across Jack's face.

"Wow!" he said, admiringly. "Wherever did you find this? It's perfect. Thank you!" Waving goodbye, Jack hurried off to attach his new mast.

"A mast and a sail," Kiara said to herself. "They shouldn't be too tricky to find." Then she sighed, remembering the weeks of searching. "Perhaps there'll be some leaves floating in the pond by Isla's house."

But when Kiara reached the pond, there were no leaves to be seen. Across the water, Kiara spotted Isla examining her boat. There were scratches running up and down the side.

"I'd painted patterns on the wood," Isla explained when Kiara walked over. "But then I went to practise in the pond. I didn't realise it was so rocky – now they are spoiled!" Isla sniffed, her eyes glittering with tears.

Kiara ran her fingers over the bumps on the boat. It looked like Isla had worked really hard on it . . .

"Here," said Kiara decisively, pulling out handfuls of shells from her pockets. "Why don't you use these to cover the scratches?"

Isla's eyes widened and she laughed in delight. "Thanks, Kiara! That's a brilliant idea."

Kiara stayed to help Isla stick the shells onto her boat, and by the time they had finished, stars were beginning to shimmer in the sky.

"Is your boat ready?" asked Isla.

Kiara tried to smile. "Oh, I don't think I'll race tomorrow after all."

"Why not?" cried Isla, shocked.

Kiara explained to a thoughtful Isla that she'd given her sail to Lizzie and her mast to Jack.

"And these shells were yours too? Oh, Kiara! I wish there was a way we could all help you, too!"

"That's okay," said Kiara, her voice wobbling a little, "At least I can cheer you all on from the bank." She stifled a yawn and said goodbye to Isla. Then she flew home, her wings heavy.

Pausing at her garden gate, Kiara looked sadly at her bare little boat with no mast or sail, still tied to the fence. "Never mind," Kiara thought bravely. "There's always next year."

The next morning hundreds of fairies lined the stream, ready for the Midsummer Boat Race. They waved banners and pointed excitedly at the line of beautiful boats bobbing in the water. Kiara wriggled through the crowd, searching for a good spot. She ran her eyes along the boats - where were Jack, Isla and Lizzie? She couldn't see her friends anywhere!

"Kiara!" called a voice from behind her.

Kiara turned and gasped as the loveliest boat she'd ever seen sailed up to the start line. It had a silver mast and a shiny leaf sail, along with flags made of Lizzie's material and oars made from Jack's old mast. Dozens of beautiful shells decorated the sides of the boat, and best of all - it was big enough for four!

Kiara hurried over and Isla helped her aboard.

"Do you like it?" Jack asked, grinning.

"We worked all night to finish it," Lizzie said, yawning. "Now we can race together!"

"It's wonderful," Kiara cried. She couldn't believe her friends had gone to all that trouble. At that moment, a shrill whistle blew. The race had begun!

As the beautiful boat rushed down the stream a huge smile spread across Kiara's face. She jumped behind the wheel, steering the boat as they skimmed over the water. The fairies on the bank were a blur, and before long Kiara and her friends could see the finish line. The crowd cheered as they sailed across it in first place.

"This was the best boat race ever!" Kiara called over the roaring crowd. "And you're the best ever friends!"

The Friendship Fairy

Written by Lucy M. George

Illustrated by Gareth Llewhellin

The Friendship Fairy

Rose wandered around the empty rooms of her new home looking for something to do. Mummy and Daddy were busy unpacking and though she'd offered to help them, they'd told her to go and play instead. But the new house felt so quiet and lonely, and anyway she didn't have anyone to play with.

Rose peered out of her bedroom window. The street was empty. She picked up the leaving book her class had made for her – it was full of photographs and funny messages.

"I miss my old friends," she sighed, looking at a picture of a smiling girl with red hair and blue eyes. "I'll never make a friend as good as Sophie ever again."

"Of course you will," said a voice from just above her head. "I'll help you!"

Rose looked up in amazement. There was something shimmering, right up high on the very top bookshelf. It was a tiny little fairy! She had a pretty blue dress, bouncy red hair, a sprinkle of freckles across her nose, and a pair of silvery wings.

"Wow!" gasped Rose. "Um, I mean hello! Who are you . . . ?" With a flutter of wings, and a flurry of sparkles, the fairy leapt from the shelf. Then she flew around the room and began to sing a beautiful song.

It went:

I'm the Friendship Fairy.

I've come to stay a while.

I'll help you meet new friends to play with,

Ones who'll make you smile.

Only you can see me,

But I promise I'll stay near,

Until you've made a true friend,

And then I'll disappear.

"But where will you go?" asked Rose.

"To help someone else, of course," said the fairy. "I'm Freya, by the way."

And with that Freya sent a shower of sparkles from her wand, which swirled all around Rose and then out of the window. The fairy fluttered down and landed on Rose's shoulder. "Now, shall we go outside and play?" she asked.

"There's no one to play with!" said Rose in surprise.

But when she looked out of the window she saw that there were two children running outside, holding a skipping rope. Just then one little girl spotted Rose in the window and waved.

"Oh!" cried Rose. She ducked out of sight, her cheeks burning. "I wish I could go and play, but what if they don't want me to join in with them?"

Freya smiled and showered Rose with more fairy dust. "Give it a try," she said. "You can do it!"

"I can!" said Rose, feeling a little braver. She walked carefully down the stairs while Freya fluttered reassuringly next to her.

Rose opened the front door a fraction, and glanced outside. She loved skipping, but her tummy was full of butterflies. Freya took Rose's hand in hers.

"You won't let go, will you?" asked Rose.

"I promise I'll be right beside you, Rose," whispered Freya. "Be brave!"

Together, they stepped outside, and Rose walked over to the girls.

"H . . . hello," she said. "I'm Rose and I'm new."

"Hello, Rose! I'm Ellie," said the girl with friendly brown eyes and bunches. "Do you like skipping? We need another person to play with us – it's no good with two."

Rose nodded. They did want her to join in after all!

They skipped all afternoon, and although no one else could see her, Freya was there the whole time.

"Will you come and play tomorrow?" asked Ellie, when it was time for tea.

"I'd love to," said Rose. "Bye!" But the next morning the sky was grey and rainy, and Rose felt all her bravery from the day before vanish. "No one will want to play today," she said in a small voice. "We should just stay inside."

"Perhaps," said Freya, "but let's give it a try first." She waved her wand and sparkling fairy magic fell onto Rose, who tingled all over and felt better instantly.

Freya flew alongside her as she ran out into the park. They found Ellie and some other children reading out loud in a tree house.

"Rose!" Ellie called down. "Come up here – we need someone to be the knight in our play."

Inside the tree house Rose met all the other children from her street. She tried very hard not to be scared. If once in a while she felt a bit nervous she knew she had Freya's magic, and her new friend Ellie always seemed to be there to help her to be brave.

With each day that passed, Rose found that she needed Freya's magic less and less. She stayed close to Ellie and soon the pair became inseparable.

A few weeks later Rose noticed another new family moving in over the road. She looked up at the window and saw a little boy watching them. She smiled and waved, but he disappeared in a flash. Rose remembered that feeling. That evening, Freya found Rose looking out of her bedroom window across the street.

"Freya, I am brave all by myself now," said Rose, "and I've made a true friend. I don't want you to go, but I think someone else needs you."

The fairy smiled at Rose. "I'm so proud of you," she said. Then with a wave of her wand she sent a shower of sparkles into the air, which made Rose feel brave about saying goodbye.

"Goodbye, Rose!" Freya called.

"Thank you, Freya!" said Rose.

The fairy leapt from the window and fluttered out into the evening sun. She flew across the street leaving a trail of sparkles behind her. Then she disappeared in through the new boy's window.

Rose waved and smiled. It was hard letting Freya go, but she knew she'd have a new friend to play with tomorrow. And she knew Freya would be there too, even if she couldn't see her.

The Cloud Fairies

Written by Lucy M. George

Illustrated by Rachel Baines

The Cloud Fairies

Long long ago, a secret fairy folk lived upon the Earth. The world then had no colour, and everything was dull and grey. But for the fairies it was like a giant canvas, and they used their magic to brighten it up. They lived to make the world more fun, and doing so made them happy.

They painted trees with greens and golds, they splashed the ocean with blues and silvers, and they dotted the mountains with bright flowers of every colour. They gave the leopard its spots and they splashed pink onto the feathers of the flamingo.

When they had finished, they chose a great big tree to live in, and settled down to admire their work. But soon the fairies realised that there was nothing left to do. They longed for another empty canvas to draw on. And so our story begins.

Cumulo and Nimbo were bored, bored, bored. They sat at the top of their tree and looked down upon some children who were watching the soft white clouds drift across the big blue sky.

"Look at those children admiring how fun we've made the world!" said Cumulo. But just then, the children said something surprising. Perhaps even a little rude.

"Clouds are so boring!" said one.

"I agree," said the other. "They are all the same!"

Cumulo and Nimbo looked up at the sky. Each cloud was perfect and fluffy. But it was true, they were all the same. The fairies looked at each other . . . Of course! Their work wasn't finished at all – the sky above them was still a huge blank canvas!

They flew to the other fairies as fast as they could.

"We have an idea!" said Cumulo.

"And everybody can join in!" said Nimbo.

They explained their plan to the other fairies, who listened, wide-eyed.

"I want to make a cloud like a racing rabbit!" cried Alto eagerly, blonde curls bouncing.

"I want to make one like a big wobbly jelly!" exclaimed Strato, beaming happily.

Soon all the fairies were chattering excitedly, each dreaming up increasingly grand ideas for the clouds they would make.

No one could get to sleep that night
but the very next morning the fairies were
up at first light. They lined up at the top of the
tree and leapt into the sky to start their journey
to the clouds. Cumulo and Nimbo led the way.

"Come on!" cried Cumulo. "We're
nearly there!"

"We're flying as fast as we can!" they cried.
"We're going so high!"

Higher and higher they climbed, their wings
beating hard in the warm summer air.

"Wow!" they cried, looking all around. "Look at them all!"

There before them, and as far as the eye could see, the sky was
filled with hundreds of identical fluffy clouds.

How beautiful they would make it!

"This looks like a good place to start," said
Nimbo, landing softly in the middle of a cloud.
The others landed gently beside him with a
PLOOMPH.

The fairies got to work immediately. They gathered huge handfuls of cloud and began to shape it, stretch it, and mould it. They used their magic to form the clouds into the most exciting shapes they could think of!

"Look, I've made a cloud shaped like a unicorn!" shouted Cumulo.

"Brilliant!" said Nimbo. "I'll make a princess to sit on it."

"I've made a whale!" said Alto.

"I've made a bigger whale!" said Strato. "And it's faster than yours! SPLASH!" Then Strato made a huge wave which covered everything.

The sky was quickly filling up with clouds shaped like every sort of thing you can imagine. Whole cities appeared as the fairies made taller and taller buildings, each trying to outdo the last. Wild animals chased each other through the air. Every fairy was busily making something.

"We did it," beamed Cumulo. "Look at the sky!"

Nimbo looked up and grinned. "It looks amazing!"

Down on Earth, the two children had woken early and they stood with their mouths open wide, watching the spectacle in the sky. "What is going on up there?" said one.

"I don't know," said the other. "But it's brilliant!"

"Look! That cloud looks like a dinosaur eating an ice-cream!" said one.

"And that one looks like a wizard riding a hippopotamus!" said the other. "That's so cool!"

As children all around the world awoke, they noticed the clouds and smiled. Not everyone saw the same things, but everyone agreed there must be a little bit of magic at work.

And what of the fairies, who lived to make the world more fun? They had never been happier. In fact, they loved it so much that they decided to stay up in the clouds. The Cloud Fairies are still up there to this very day, making the world a bit more fun . . . And if you don't believe me, just take a look up at the sky!

The Toy Fairy

Written by Josephine Collins

Illustrated by Amanda Gulliver

The Toy Fairy

It was a bright, sparkling night, and the Toy Fairy was busy working her special magic. She landed softly on a window ledge and pulled a smart green train with shiny new paint from her sack of mended toys. With a wave of her wand and a flash of glittering light, she sent it zooming back into the little boy's bedroom. He gasped with delight at the sight of his beloved toy.

The Toy Fairy watched with pleasure as he started playing. It was such a heart-warming sight that she decided to stay for a little while longer.

"He looks so happy!" she whispered in her tiny, tinkling voice. "I truly have the best job in all the world." Then the Toy Fairy sighed, and her little face dropped. "If only I wasn't so shy, perhaps I could go in and play too." But the Toy Fairy had many other toys to mend and children to visit. Shrugging her shoulders firmly, she turned away from the window, grasped her sack of toys, and zoomed off high into the moonlit sky to finish her deliveries.

Later that night, when all the toys had been returned, it was time to collect up the day's wishes. Peeping in through a little girl's window, the Toy Fairy spotted a broken doll waiting for her. "I know that doll!" she gasped. "That's the first toy I ever fixed. I recognise her buttons!"

But that was a long time ago, and the doll was broken again from years of being loved and played with. Her arm and dress were torn and her once soft hair was nearly worn away.

The Toy Fairy watched as the little girl who had wished for her help, hugged the doll tight. "I hope the Toy Fairy comes and makes you all better, just like Mummy said she would," she whispered to the doll, as she turned over and closed her eyes. The Toy Fairy waited until the little girl had fallen asleep, then she waved her wand and the broken doll was transported to her sack. In its place she left a tiny glittering note . . .

Your toy is with the Toy Fairy and she will return it as good as new!

"I'll be back tomorrow . . ." whispered the Toy Fairy to the sleeping girl. And with a fluttering of wings, she was gone, flying high across the twinkling night sky.

As soon as she reached her fairy workshop, the Toy Fairy began searching through the towering shelves of colourful materials. She had everything she could possibly need to make the doll as good as new once again.

The Toy Fairy got to work at once – she chose just the right kind of stuffing for the doll's arm, something soft to make her hair, and the perfect fabric to mend her dress. Then she worked long into the night – stitching and polishing, mending and patching, until at last the doll was transformed.

The next night, full of anticipation, the Toy Fairy returned to the little girl's window. She waved her magic wand and the air filled with sparkles as the doll whizzed through the air, back to the little girl's bed. The Toy Fairy watched hopefully. She knew she ought to leave, but she so wanted to see the little girl's face when she discovered her doll.

The Toy Fairy waited and waited until at last she sighed and turned away. She was just about to leap into the sky when a delighted voice behind her whispered, "Are you the Toy Fairy?" It was the little girl!

The Toy Fairy nodded shyly. She didn't know what to say; she'd never spoken to a person before.

"Thank you so much for mending my doll," said the little girl, smiling at her. "My name is Emily. Would you like to come in?"

The Toy Fairy hesitated. "Yes please," she said finally, and fluttered through the open window.

"Wow! You can really fly!" cried Emily. "Shall we play a game?"

"I'm not sure I can," said the Toy Fairy. "I mean, I think I would like to, only I've never played a game before."

"Really?" Emily laughed in surprise. "But you're the Toy Fairy! Surely you're allowed to play with the toys sometimes."

"That's true!" giggled the Toy Fairy. "I guess I never had anyone to play with before."

So Emily showed the Toy Fairy how she gave her doll supper, and then they read her stories together and tucked her up in her cosy cot.

"It's time for me to go!" the Toy Fairy said, sadly. "But I promise I'll visit again soon!"

After that night, the Toy Fairy visited Emily whenever she had the chance. Emily showed her how to play all sorts of games. Sometimes they played with the dolls' house (the Toy Fairy was just the right size to fit inside the house with the dolls!), and they were really good at playing dragons and knights, and princesses and fairies too.

As the Toy Fairy grew braver she made friends with many of the little girls and boys whose toys she mended. But she never forgot Emily.

Then one night, Emily said, "I have a surprise for you!" She ran over to her jewellery box and searched through it to find a tiny ring. "This is for you! A friendship bracelet for my very best friend!"

"Thank you!" said the Toy Fairy, beaming as Emily carefully slipped it over her hand. And as they played and laughed together, the Toy Fairy thought she must be the luckiest fairy ever! She had never been happier. Not only did she love her job mending toys, but now she got to share them with some very special children. And best of all she had Emily – her very first friend.

Lily's Wish

Written by Becky Davies

Illustrated by Kim Barnes

Lily's Wish

Lily hummed to herself as she put a final stitch through the tiny clover leaves, and tied a knot in her silk. "Perfect!" she said. She leaned back in her chair to admire the gloves she had just finished making. Every leaf was embroidered daintily, and they looked beautiful.

Just then, Lily caught sight of another fairy zooming purposefully past the workshop window – it was a scout fairy. Lily sighed. How she wished she could be a scout! They were brave and fast, and spent their days flying far and wide across the countryside collecting flowers and trinkets. Only the biggest, strongest fairies could fly as far as they did. Lily's wings were so tiny that they would only take her round the garden before she felt tired out!

Lily was the smallest of all the fairies, and with her little fingers she made an excellent seamstress. She could stitch even the most delicate of materials! She dearly loved her job working with leaves and stems, petals and silks, but often she thought how wonderful it would be to see them growing in the countryside. What an adventure that would be!

"Lily!" cried her friend Crystal. "Come quickly. Hazel's got some big news!"

Lily flew over to where the rest of the fairies were gathered, and stood on her tiptoes to peep over their shoulders.

"Now then," said Hazel importantly. "This letter contains a request from none other than Princess Rose herself! Her Royal Highness has asked us for some new clothes for her wardrobe and," she paused for dramatic effect, "will be visiting us in person to collect them."

The fairies gasped in amazement.

Dear Fairies

Princess Rose xx x

"It's a huge honour," continued Hazel, "and we will have the finest materials ready for you to work with in the morning. We must all do our very best for the princess!"

The fairies fluttered out of the workshop in gossiping groups.

"What are you going to make for Princess Rose?" Crystal asked Lily eagerly. "I'm thinking of making her a new silk-lined cloak."

Lily's mind was a whirl of ideas, but she couldn't choose between them. What could be special enough for a princess who has everything?

Lily reached her house and waved goodbye to Crystal. She lingered at her front door and gazed up at the twilight sky. She had a funny feeling that tomorrow might bring the adventure she'd been wishing for.

The next morning Lily arrived at the workshop early, keen to get a head start on her ideas. But the materials table was already buzzing with excited fairies, all eager to make something special to impress the princess.

"I'm going to make her a new dress!" cried Luna, rushing past with armfuls of pink rose petals.

"This will make an adorable pair of slippers," said Astrid, grabbing a crimson poppy.

There were so many beautiful things to choose between! How would Lily decide? She needed to make something extraordinary, something that the princess wouldn't have already.

Her eyes found a small pile of wicker branches that no one else had wanted. Perhaps she could come up with something unique using those?

The other fairies had already set to work, their pine needles swooping in and out of leaves with strands of finest spider silk. They weaved stems and pleated petals to perfection. They began to make acorn hats, daisy skirts and ball gowns made from bluebells. Lily breathed in the smells with wonder, her mind full of images of colourful flowers and endless meadows.

As she glanced around the workshop at the bustling fairies, Lily noticed scraps of material lying on the floor unused. A piece of silk here.

Some twine there. She felt sad about the waste. Then suddenly, she had an idea! She collected the wicker branches and scraps quickly and set to work at once.

"What's that you're making, Lily?" asked Hazel, peering at the wicker she was weaving and the heap of different materials.

"It's a secret, but it's going to be amazing," Lily assured her. And she hoped it would be. She stayed in the workshop after the others had left, sewing long into the night. She so hoped Princess Rose would love her special gift!

The very next day trumpets announced the arrival of the royal carriage, and the fairies marvelled as Princess Rose entered the workshop. She had long auburn hair, gleaming blue eyes, and a beaming smile as bright as starlight.

"Welcome, your majesty!" said Hazel, curtseying. "We do hope you're pleased with what we've made."

"I can't wait to see it all!" the princess replied warmly.

Hazel led the princess to each fairy in turn, as they nervously presented their creations.

"Beautiful!" she exclaimed, as the rose petal dress was laid in front of her.

"A perfect fit!" she said, as she tried on the poppy petal slippers. She gave each dressmaker a special thank you, and soon their faces were all pink with pride. Finally, she reached Lily.

Lily twisted her hands anxiously as Princess Rose approached.

"And this is Lily, your highness," said Hazel.

"Hello, Lily!" said the princess cheerfully. "What have you made?"

"Erm, actually," said Lily, blushing, "I was hoping you wouldn't mind coming outside . . ."

The princess looked puzzled, but motioned for Lily to lead the way. The other fairies followed curiously.

Around the back of the workshop there stood a beautiful hot-air balloon! It was sewn from patches of different fabrics; shiny yellow buttercups, creamy white daisy petals and sheets of silk embroidered with lavender. Each patch was perfectly stitched together, and hanging below the balloon was a beautiful wicker basket!

Princess Rose paused, and then clapped her hands in delight. "Why, this is marvellous!" she cried. "But how did you think of it?"

"I know you can't wear it, but I kept thinking how wonderful it would be to fly with the birds to the treetops and see the meadows full of flowers like the scouts can and, well, I thought you might like that too."

"I think this is the most special present I have ever been given," said the princess solemnly. "And I think we've found a new scout!"

The workshop erupted into surprised chatter, and Lily's mouth fell open. "But . . . You can't mean me? I'm no good at flying!"

The princess smiled. "You know, scouts don't just have to be strong," she said. "They also have to be creative, and resourceful. You've shown all of these things, Lily. I couldn't think of a better scout." Lily could hardly believe her ears! "You can make your own special hot-air balloon and you'll be able to fly as far as you like!" the princess beamed. "Now, shall we go for a ride?"

The other fairies cheered as Lily and Princess Rose took off in the balloon, and Lily thought she might burst with happiness as she began her first ever adventure.

Grumpy Grisabel

Written by Becky Davies

Illustrated by Sarah Jennings

Grumpy Grisabel

"Pesky fairies again!" cried Grisabel. She crumpled up the pink invitation that had just been posted through her letterbox, and jammed her pointy black hat on her head. "Everywhere I turn there's another fairy tea party full of pink pests." She grabbed her cloak, slammed her front door behind her, and stomped through the woods.

Grisabel was in a bad mood, but for her that wasn't unusual. She was a grumpy witch by nature, and the longer she lived in Bluebell Wood the grumpier she became. The reason was clear . . . "Fairies!" she roared again, tearing fistfuls of sparkly ribbon from a nearby tree. As well as being her home, Bluebell Wood was positively packed with fairies.

Grisabel had tolerated them when they had first settled amongst the gnarled trees, but as time passed more fairies had joined them and Grisabel's patience had worn out.

She was the only witch for miles around, and she was surrounded by glitter and sparkles and frivolous talk. "They can't even do real magic," Grisabel grumbled to herself. "All they do is faff about with flowers and make ridiculous rainbows."

Without realising, Grisabel had stomped her way into a ring of toadstools. She heard voices and realised her mistake. Quickly, she hid herself behind a nearby bush.

Gathered in the midst of the toadstools was a jolly group of fairies, enjoying a picnic amongst the trees.

"I do declare this is the most wonderful picnic yet!" trilled Ruby, as she munched on a tiny star-shaped sandwich.

"Such a marvellous spread!" agreed Martha, reaching for an icing-covered pastry.

"And the decorations look superb," added Christa happily.

Grisabel peered round her bush. She could see jellies and trifles, and stacks of cupcakes with strawberry icing. The trees had been adorned with

streamers, and absolutely everything was pink. "Yuck!" Grisabel muttered.

She was just about to sneak off when she heard her name mentioned by one of the fairies. "Did you give Grisabel the invitation, Ruby?" asked Christa brightly. "She should be here by now!"

"Yes I did," replied Ruby, then she hesitated. "I posted it through her letterbox. I could hear her inside. She didn't sound too happy."

"Oh dear," said Christa. "I really hoped she'd come this time. How do we show her we just want to be friends?"

Grisabel had heard enough, and slipped away. "Humph," she grumbled, rubbing at a crick in her back. "Be friends with those dancing dimwits! Not likely!" She continued through the forest, muttering angrily to herself all the while. She was so absorbed that she almost ran into two small children, who had been picking fruit in the woods.

The children were dressed as fairies, complete with glittering wings. They looked up at Grisabel, taking in her striped tights, crooked nose and pointy hat. Before Grisabel could even open her mouth to say hello, they screamed.

"Help!" they cried. "The witch has come to get us!" They dropped their baskets of apples and ran shrieking through the trees.

Grisabel sighed sadly. "That's it!" she said. "I've had enough! I won't stay in this wood one minute longer." She marched decisively back the way she had come. "Farewell ribbon," she cried, "goodbye glitter, and good riddance to fairies!"

She rounded a corner, and suddenly saw a frilly heap in front of her on the path. It was one of the children! The poor thing was crying quietly, and turned to Grisabel in fright.

Grisabel stopped where she was. "It's okay, child," she said. "Don't be afraid." But the little girl only cried harder.

"I won't hurt you," said Grisabel. "See?" She pulled out her wand slowly, and gave it a flick. A toy rabbit appeared and floated gently over to the girl. She stopped crying and hesitated for a moment, before reaching out to take it. "What's wrong?" asked Grisabel.

"I twisted my ankle," sniffed the girl quietly. "My friend Sarah's gone for help."

"I see. And what's your name?"

"Jennifer," she said into the rabbit's fur.

Grisabel moved a little closer, then she knelt down and waved her wand again.

"My ankle," cried Jennifer, surprised. "You fixed it! But I thought witches were mean and scary?"

"Yes, well . . . " mumbled Grisabel, but before she could say more the little girl had thrown her arms around her neck.

"Thank you," she whispered. Then she stood up slowly and tested her ankle. "Sarah will never believe me when I tell her. Goodbye!" And with that, she skipped off.

Grisabel smiled to herself, popping her wand in her pocket as she got to her feet. Then she noticed Jennifer's basket of apples, lying forgotten. "Wait!" she cried, snatching up the basket and running after her.

But she hadn't gone far when she tripped over a tree root and landed in a heap on the forest floor. "Bother!" she said, examining her broken glasses. She reached for her wand to repair them, only to find that it had snapped clean in half when she fell.

"Double bother!" she said, looking around at the trees. To Grisabel they were a mass of blurred shapes. How on earth was she going to be able to find her way home?

Grisabel took a deep breath and started walking in what she hoped was the right direction. But after she had tripped over her fourth tree root she gave up hope, and slumped forlornly against a tree.

It began to rain, and a single tear rolled down her warty nose. But just then, she felt a tiny tug at her sleeve, and something was placed into her hand.

She looked down and saw her glasses and wand, both fixed as good as new! It was the fairies – they had come to rescue her! Grisabel was lost for words.

"We mended them for you," beamed Ruby. "It was easy to fit the pieces together, and then they just needed a sprinkling of fairy dust."

"Oh thank you, thank you!" Grisabel cried. "You wonderful, clever, kind creatures! But . . . " she gasped, "why would you help me when I'm always so horrid to you?"

The fairies smiled at her. "That's what friends are for!" they said.

Grisabel went to bed that night in a thoughtful mood, and when she woke in the morning she felt somehow different. As she was about to leave her cottage, she noticed two new pieces of mail lying on her doormat. Picking them up, she saw that one was an invitation to the next fairy picnic. Instead of screwing it up, she pinned it to her notice board carefully before looking at the other piece of paper. It was a drawing of her, from the little girl! Grisabel stuck it on her wall at once, and stood back to admire it. "You know," she said, "I think I'll stay in Bluebell Wood after all."

The Birthday Surprise

Written by Gillian Hibbs

Illustrated by Kim Barnes

The Birthday Surprise

"I'd like a one-hundred-layered – no, a one-THOUSAND-layered birthday cake, covered in colour-changing icing and sprinkles and sparkles," Princess Florence announced to her worried-looking maid. "I also want an orchard of trees that grow toffees – oh, and a herd of hula-hooping hippos. Better than those fire-breathing ponies from last year; they were rubbish!" Princess Florence was demanding at the best of times, but never more so than for her birthday party.

The maid flew to the great hall at top speed to pass on the princess's latest demands. Florence's birthday was tomorrow, and she kept asking for more things!

"There's a limit to what even magic can do!" said Mrs Potts, the cook. "She gets worse every year!"

"You'd think she'd be happy with nothing to do all day but order people around," said Billy, who looked after the animals.

The castle was in complete chaos, with panicked fairies waving their wands furiously and spells flying everywhere. They were making a terrible racket.

"That's it!" cried the Fairy King. "All of you, stop! This birthday business is getting out of hand." The fairies all stopped at once and turned to face him.

"We're worried about Princess Florence's ungrateful behaviour," said the Fairy Queen.

"We want to teach her the value of magic," continued the king. "That's why we're going to do something we've never done before." He paused. "We're going to put a spell on the castle, which will stop magic working for one day!"

A whisper of shock spread amongst the fairies. "No magic?!" they cried.

The queen raised her hands and they fell quiet. "Please trust us," she said. "We're going to need everybody's help."

The morning of Florence's birthday began like any other. "Happy birthday to Florence, happy birthday to yoooou!" chorused the king and queen. "Good morning, darling! There's a surprise waiting for you in the kitchen!"

"How strange! I've never even *been* to the kitchen! They must want to show me my birthday cake," thought Florence, as she fluttered down the stairs. Mrs Potts was waiting for her at the door.

"Quickly now, Princess," said Mrs Potts, "one thousand layers won't bake themselves you know!"

"What are you talking about?" Florence asked as an apron was thrown over her head and a wooden spoon thrust into her hand. "I'm not baking. Why haven't you just used magic?"

But Mrs Potts had flown off to fetch the icing sugar.

"Fine," said Florence, "I'll do it myself!" She pulled out her wand and gave it a wave. Nothing happened. "What's going on?" she demanded.

"Magic doesn't seem to be working this morning, Princess," said Mrs Potts, bustling back. "We'll just have to do our best without it. It *is* your birthday, after all."

Florence grumbled as she mixed, but gradually she stopped noticing her aching wrist. She chattered away as the cooks prepared delicious smelling dishes all around her. By the time she had finished she had egg in her hair, flour down her front and icing on her nose – but the cake looked wonderful.

"Just another nine hundred and ninety-nine layers to go!" said Mrs Potts.

Florence looked at the cake she had baked. "Perhaps I don't need one thousand layers after all. This one is perfect!"

"Come along then, Princess," said Mrs Potts, briskly. "I know someone who needs your help in the garden."

"The garden!" Florence protested. "Can't I stay here? I'll get dirty!"

But Mrs Potts whisked her outside.

"Here you go, Princess," said Mr Rake, the gardener, as he passed Florence a pot of glue and a brush. "We need to stick all these toffees onto the branches of the trees."

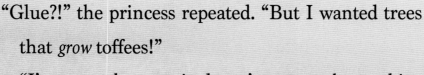

"Glue?!" the princess repeated. "But I wanted trees that *grow* toffees!"

"I'm sorry, but magic doesn't seem to be working this morning, and without magic that's impossible," Mr Rake sighed. "Some things can be grown without magic of course, but not toffees."

Florence waved her wand again, just to check that Mr Rake was telling the truth. "I hope someone's trying to fix this!" she said grumpily, as she picked up a toffee and started gluing.

After she'd been sticking toffees on for a while, Florence said, "I didn't actually know you could grow things without magic . . . What kind of things?"

Mr Rake smiled. He loved talking about growing things. He showed

Florence his beds of bright marigolds and tulips, then proudly led her to
his prize rosebushes.

"Wow!" said Florence, stroking the delicate petals of the beautiful red
roses. "And you grew these without magic? They're amazing!"

When Mr Rake offered his roses for her party instead of the trees
Florence was delighted. "Great!" said Mr Rake, "Just one more thing to do!"
And he bustled her off to the swamp to meet Billy. Florence didn't even know
they *had* a swamp, but Mr Rake pointed her in the right direction.

Florence found Billy sobbing next to a pair of very lazy-looking hippos, with a pile of hula-hoops lying next to them.

"It's no use without magic!" he sniffed. "They won't do anything I say!"

One of the hippos let out a loud grunt, as if he was agreeing, and Florence giggled. "Here, I'll help," she said, and Billy smiled gratefully. She held the hoop as Billy tried to push the hippo into it. But instead it sat down, splattering mud everywhere!

Florence burst into laughter and Billy joined in, until they were both clutching their sides. "I don't think these hippos are really the hula-hooping type!" she howled.

Florence didn't even reach for her wand this time to check the magic – she realized she liked the hippos as they were. Instead, she and Billy played with the hula-hoops themselves and even though they were covered in swamp mud, Florence was having too much fun to care.

In fact she completely lost track of time . . . "Oops! I forgot about my birthday party!" she squeaked, waving goodbye to Billy as she flew towards the castle.

Florence speedily changed into her party clothes and whizzed down to greet her guests. The beaming princess made sure that her new friends got a taste of the cake she'd baked, while she showed off Mr Rake's roses and made them all laugh by telling them about the unhelpful hippos.

The king and queen beamed with pride, and winked at the castle staff. It seemed their plan had worked! Florence was happier than they had ever seen her.

"Happy birthday, darling!" whispered the queen after the last of the guests had left, hugging her smiling daughter. Then she waved her wand, and instantly the castle was sparkling clean.

"The magic's back!" cried Princess Florence, seizing her wand and running outside. "Good! There's one more thing I want!"

The fairies looked at each other nervously. Oh dear. What now? But they needn't have worried. With a flick of Florence's wand, multi-coloured fireworks filled the sky!

THANK YOU!

"I really mean it," Florence said. "Thank you, my friends, for the best birthday ever!"

Maeve's Wonderful Workshop

Written by Amelia Hepworth

Illustrated by Maurizia Rubino

Maeve's Wonderful Workshop

Everyone knows that fairies are good at everything. They're always neat and tidy, with shiny hair and sparkly dresses. They love jewels and glitter, they adore parties and flower arranging, and they're especially good at baking. But Maeve wasn't like other fairies . . .

"Good morning, Maeve!" trilled Belle and Poppy merrily, as they sprinkled shiny drops of dew on to the delicate hedgerow flowers. "Where are you off to at this time in the morning?"

"Hi Poppy, hi Belle!" called Maeve, clattering to a stop next to her friends. She landed so hard all the dew bounced off the flowers. "Whoops! Sorry! I'm so clumsy," she laughed apologetically. The other fairies smiled – this kind of thing was always happening to Maeve. "I was just on the way to my workshop," she said. "I've nearly finished the project I'm working on."

"Oh, well Belle and I are just about to go and do some baking for tonight's Fairy Ball, if you'd like to join us?" said Poppy.

"Everyone's making something to take along," added Belle in her soft, silvery voice. "You could go to your workshop afterwards!"

"Ummm . . . sure, that sounds lovely!" replied Maeve. "I guess I could come along for a bit."

So the three friends fluttered off to the kitchens and before long they were up to their wings in icing sugar and candied sweets. Poppy baked perfect heart-shaped cookies with pretty pink icing. Belle made colourful cupcakes with rainbow glitter and mountains of marshmallows. And Maeve made . . . Well, no one was quite sure what Maeve had made.

"Oh dear!" groaned Maeve. "I'm no good at baking. I wish I could be more like you two."

The other fairies hugged her. "It doesn't matter – we love you just the way you are. And anyway, we've made enough for all of us," they told her.

But Maeve just sighed and looked sadly at the mess she'd made. "I'd better go," she said, peeling off her floury apron.

"We'll see you tonight." called Poppy after her. "It's going to be so much fun!"

Maeve turned and smiled at her friends. "Of course. See you later," she called back. And then, in the blink of an eye, she was gone.

Later that day, the fairies were getting ready for the ball in Poppy's bedroom. "What do you think Maeve gets up to in that workshop of hers?" wondered Belle as she slipped into her pretty pink ball dress. It had hundreds of sparkling jewels sewn into the skirt and it had taken her days to make.

"I can't imagine," said Poppy, fastening the buttons on her shiny silver slippers. "No one's ever been inside. It's a mystery!"

Just then there was a knock at the door. The other fairies had arrived! They were whisked away in carriages, straight to the grand ballroom where the fairies stared in awe at magnificent chandeliers, towering flower arrangements and endless tables laden with delicious treats.

"It's spectacular!" whispered Poppy. And she squeaked with delight as the band began to play. "Come on, Belle, let's dance!"

They waltzed and twirled merrily until they became dizzy. "Goodness!" laughed Belle, looking around her. "I'm having so much fun. But where's Maeve? I haven't seen her all night."

"I think we ought to go and find her," said Poppy. "I expect she's at her workshop. She wouldn't want to miss the ball!"

The fairies set off, and before long they arrived at a pretty red door with an acorn knocker. They peered through the window and sure enough there was Maeve, humming away happily as she worked. She answered the door looking flustered.

"I'm so sorry!" she exclaimed. "I got caught up in my work and completely forgot about the ball! I've just finished – I'll be ready in two minutes." And she disappeared behind a curtain.

"Wow!" exclaimed Belle as they stepped inside. "It's wonderful in here!"

"Look!" cried Poppy in wonder. In the centre of the workshop there stood a beautiful wooden sculpture of a magnificent swan. It was twice as tall as the fairies, with elegant wings spread out above their heads.

Just then Maeve reappeared holding a torn ball dress. "I ripped my dress trying to put it on!" she said to her friends in a small voice. "And I don't have anything to bring to the party!"

Maeve sat down in a heap. "I'm a rubbish fairy! Why can't I just be like everybody else?"

Poppy and Belle hugged their friend and dried her tears.

"Ummm . . . did you make this, Maeve?" Belle asked, looking up at the swan.

Maeve nodded shyly. "It's nothing really," she sniffed. "Just a hobby."

"It's beautiful," said Poppy. "You're so talented!"

"I have an idea," said Belle excitedly. "You must bring it to the Fairy Ball! It would be the perfect thing. Oh please say we can!"

"I'm not sure . . ." said Maeve uncertainly, but Poppy and Belle insisted. Poppy helped Maeve into her dress and lent her a pretty shawl to cover the rip. Then they set off for the ball.

By the time the friends returned to the ballroom with Maeve's creation the party was in full swing. Fairies bustled to and fro with jugs of frothy lemonade, and the band was playing a jolly tune.

"What if people think it's silly?" worried Maeve, her cheeks flaming red. But Belle and Poppy were having none of it. They marched into the ballroom pushing the swan ahead of them and all the fairies turned to stare. A hush fell and Maeve's cheeks burned brighter than ever. Then the room erupted in excited chatter. Everyone wanted to know who had made the magnificent statue. Maeve was the toast of the Fairy Ball!

As she crept into bed later that night with her feet sore from all the dancing Maeve was the happiest fairy alive.

The next morning, Maeve had just started work on a new project when there was a knock at her workshop door. "That'll be Poppy," she thought, "come to collect her shawl." But when she opened the door it wasn't Poppy at all. It was a queue of eager-looking fairies!

"We've come to learn how to make sculptures!" said the first fairy.

"Yes, please will you teach us?" added another. "We want to be just like you!"

"I'd be delighted!" said Maeve. She glowed with happiness as she started to teach the excited fairies how to work with wood. She might not be like everyone else, but perhaps she was good at something after all.

The Secret Fairy Door

Written by Juliet Groom

Illustrated by Kim Barnes

The Secret Fairy Door

"Georgie! Come see!" called Eva. "Look what I've found!"

Georgie raced over to where Eva was sitting, gazing at a perfect
miniature door that had appeared on the wall of their treehouse. It had a
pretty pink knocker and it even had a keyhole, just made for a tiny key.

"It must be a fairy door!" Eva whispered. "It means the fairies can come through from Fairyland to visit us, Georgie! They will live right here in our treehouse. They'll be so happy!"

"It's amazing, Eva," said Georgie. "But we've never seen any fairies before – even when we left them pictures and poems, and cakes we baked ourselves!" Georgie sniffed. "I'm not sure there are any fairies living in Hawthorn Forest at all. I'm not even sure it is a real fairy door," she said. "If they don't appear soon then I think we should give our cakes to the robin who lives in our tree instead. He visits us every day!"

Eva laughed, giving her little sister a hug. "The fairies are there, you just have to be patient. They're very shy, you know."

Georgie sighed. Being patient was the hardest thing. How she wished she could see a fairy – just once!

"I know! Let's bring the doormat from our dolls' house to put outside the door. It will make the fairies feel welcome," smiled Eva. "There! Now, how about we bake some biscuits for the fairies AND for your robin? Race you home!" And off they rushed.

Inside the treehouse, all appeared quiet. But if you looked very carefully, you might have seen tiny figures darting back and forth through the fairy door. And if you listened very closely, you might have heard tiny voices laughing as the fairies excitedly explored their new home . . .

Spring turned to summer and the forest filled with flowers. School finished and Georgie and Eva spent long days up in their treehouse, reading and playing games. Eva baked seed cakes for the fairies, and every day she made something for their tiny house. "Look, Georgie, isn't this perfect?" she said, placing a miniature rocking chair outside the fairy door. "You know, I'm sure that there are fairies living here."

"No there aren't!" said Georgie crossly. "We've been here every day for weeks and we haven't seen a single one! I don't believe the fairy door works at all." And she stomped to the window to feed Charlie, the robin. He was always friendly. He hopped right up to her outstretched hand, and pecked at the seed cake in her palm.

"Don't be cross, Georgie," said Eva. "I've been reading about fairies, and they don't show themselves to humans unless you really need their help. Look, Mum got us a new colouring book. Shall we have a go?"

The girls coloured together, then ate their picnic lunch. Eva read them stories until at last, drowsy in the warm sunlight, they both fell fast asleep.

Eva dreamed of fairies building houses for the animals: fabulous houses with beds for rabbits and robins. It was a funny, happy dream, but then something went wrong. The fairies were calling to her. "Eva! Eva! Wake up!"

Eva awoke with a jump. The sun was fading; she'd been asleep for ages! "Wake up, sleepyhead," said Eva, yawning and turning to look at her sister. But Georgie wasn't in the treehouse, and she wasn't outside. She had gone!

"Georgie!" shouted Eva loudly. The girls knew they weren't allowed to wander off alone. Mum and Dad had made them promise that whenever they went to the treehouse, they'd always stay together.

Where could Georgie have gone? How was Eva ever going to find her? The forest was enormous!

"Georgieeee!" Eva shouted through the tree house window, her eyes brimming with tears. She shivered. What if something bad had happened to her? Just then she heard something. The softest whisper.

"Eva! Over here!" Spinning round, Eva gasped. She couldn't believe her eyes! Fairies! Three beautiful, tiny fairies! "Come with us," they called. "We know where Georgie is! We'll take you."

Eva zoomed down her ramp, following the fairies. Faster and faster she sped along the path, deeper into the forest. "Georgie!" Eva called. "Oh, please tell me she's OK!" "Not much farther now," said one of the fairies. Gritting her teeth, Eva raced up the hill in the darkening evening. And then she heard a small voice in the distance.

"Eva! Eva!" It was Georgie!

Eva rushed over to her sister and hugged her tight. "I was so worried about you!" she murmured.

"I'm sorry, Eva!" Georgie wailed. "I know I'm not supposed to go out on my own but I was so sure that I'd seen a fairy. I tried running after it but I fell and hurt my ankle . . ."

"Shh, shh, it's OK. Everything will be all right now," said Eva gently. "I'm here. And look who else is!"

As Georgie turned, one of the fairies fluttered down and kissed her cheek. "Wow!" Georgie gasped, her tears stopping instantly. "You ARE real! You're really real!"

"We are," the fairy whispered. "We've been there all summer, in your cosy treehouse."

"We love all the things you brought us," the others giggled. "You've been so kind! And we like the pictures you painted for us, and your cakes are delicious!"

"The door!" Georgie laughed. "Eva, you were right! The fairies have been there all along! You're the cleverest sister ever, Eva!"

And with Georgie on her lap, Eva followed their fairy friends along the forest path to home.

"Thank you," the girls called as they reached their front door and waved goodbye to the tiny fairies. "Thank you so much! We'll see you soon!"

"We'll always be there, looking out for you," the fairies promised.

"As soon as my ankle is better Eva and I will bake the best fairy cakes ever," laughed Georgie. "Just for you!"

The Springtime Ball

Written by Juliet Groom

Illustrated by Gail Yerrill

The Springtime Ball

It was the first day of spring and down in the woods, tiny voices rang out in joyful song:

> "Spring is here, the sun shines bright,
> Warming winter woods with light.
> Wakey, wakey, one and all.
> Join us for the Springtime Ball!"

Poppy, Daisy and Amber darted through the air, sprinkling the woods with golden fairy dust. As the magic sparkles drifted down, leaves uncurled and flowers blossomed.

"Look at the colours!" laughed Poppy. "I haven't seen anything this bright through all of winter."

"Or felt anything so soft!" smiled her friend Daisy. "Even the smallest snowflake isn't as soft as the petals of flowers! I so love spring," she said, stretching her arms in the warm air.

"Let's go and wake the animals!" cried Amber. "They've been sleeping all winter and I can't wait a moment longer to see them again!"

The three fairies tiptoed through the grass to where the animals had been hibernating. "Wake up, Hettie!" they called.

Snuffling and sniffing, Hettie Hedgehog peeped her head out of her winter nest. "Is it springtime already?" she yawned.

"Yes! And we've missed you!" Amber smiled, stroking her velvety nose. "You must come to the Springtime Ball tomorrow. It'll be the best party ever!"

"We should make decorations," said Daisy excitedly to her friends, as they left Hettie's nest. "Wake up, wake up! Come fly with us!" she called to the ladybirds, butterflies and bees. "There's no time to lose. The ball is tomorrow night, and you're all invited! We must get ready."

Everyone helped out, and soon the air hummed as the bees buzzed in the sunshine. They brought piles of daisies that the fairies wove into chains to hang from the branches in the clearing.

"Now *we're* as busy as bees!" laughed Poppy as she threaded the delicate flowers through fresh green stalks.

"Look!" called Amber. "It's the dragonflies! They're bringing rose petals for our ballgowns!"

After they had finished with the decorations, the three friends joined the other fairies as they made beautiful ballgowns from the delicate petals. They sewed the dresses with tiny embroidery stitches, adding golden seeds, silvery pearls and glass beads all the colours of the rainbow. They looked incredible!

"Let's go and see how the others are doing with the baking," said Poppy, as she finished her last stitch. "I can't wait to see the cakes!" And so they hung up their glittering gowns and flew off to the kitchens.

They peeped through the doors, and saw butterflies helping the fairies pipe icing on to cakes and biscuits. Each of them wore a tiny chef's hat, and as they worked they sang happy songs:

"Stir and whisk and mix and bake.
Big and small, we'll all have cake!"

"Wow!" whispered Amber. "We'll never eat all these treats!"

The fairies all worked late into the night, sewing, baking and decorating. By the time they went to bed everything was ready.

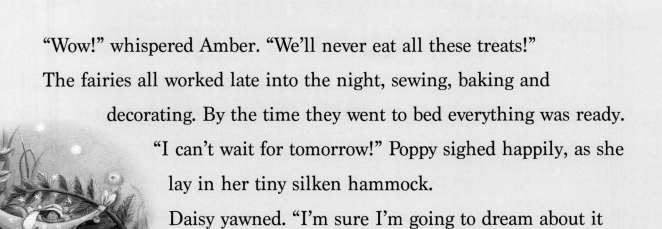

"I can't wait for tomorrow!" Poppy sighed happily, as she lay in her tiny silken hammock.

Daisy yawned. "I'm sure I'm going to dream about it tonight! Night-night, Poppy! Night, Amber! Sleep tight!"

But when the fairies woke the next morning, they had a terrible surprise. The skies were dark and rain pitter-pattered through the wood, settling on the ground in big puddles.

"Oh dear!" gasped Poppy. "We can't let the rain ruin the Springtime Ball! We must do something!"

"Don't worry, I've got an idea!" said Amber. "The sun is still up there, high above the clouds. With a bit of help we can send these rain clouds away and our party will be perfect. Come with me!" And she leapt into the air.

Higher and higher the three friends flew, up amongst the tree tops. Then Amber whistled a bright song, over and over until at last the fairies heard it: an answering trill of birdsong. It was faint at first, but soon it became louder, with running notes that called to them: tu-tu-a-wee! And then the birds arrived, flashing through the sky in a blur of blue.

"Chellie! Jasper! Charlie!" Amber called to them. "Thank goodness we found you! Could you help us? We need to make a rainbow, and chase these clouds far away. We can't fly high enough ourselves, but with your help we can take our magic into the skies."

"Of course!" chirped the birds brightly. "Anything for you!"

And so the fairies climbed up on to the backs of the bluebirds. Holding gently to the downy feathers they flew higher than ever before, up, up through the clouds.

"Wow!" cried Daisy. "I never knew birds could fly so high! It's amazing!" Each fairy sprinkled their magic fairy dust behind her. It made a trail that arced and sparkled across the sky and then, magically, burst into colour.

A glorious rainbow glowed up above and slowly the clouds drifted apart, and the sun peeped through. The fairies cheered. They had done it!

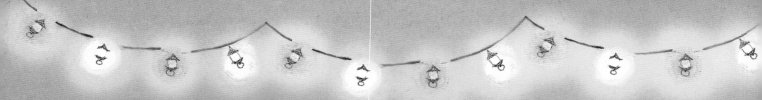

"Thank you, Chellie! Thank you, Jasper and Charlie!" called Poppy. "That was brilliant! You will join us at the ball, won't you?" And together they all flew back to the woods through the warm spring sunshine.

Back home, the party guests were gathering. Fairies flew about collecting the last few things, giggling with excitement and anticipation. Spider Sam and his jolly jazz band started to play vibrant music with harps and trumpets and a tiny drum kit. At last, the ball had begun!

Fairies twirled and butterflies in top hats bobbed through the air. Everyone ate cake and sang songs until the sky grew dim and fairy lanterns twinkled in the trees.

"I'm so happy, Poppy!" smiled Daisy, as she spun around.

"This has been the most exciting day and the most wonderful ball!" Amber added.

"Yes," laughed Poppy. "It has. I shall remember it for ever!"

Favourite Fairy Stories
An Illustrated Treasury

LITTLE TIGER PRESS LTD
an imprint of the Little Tiger Group
1 Coda Studios, 189 Munster Road,
London SW6 6AW
www.littletiger.co.uk

Published in Great Britain 2017
This volume copyright © Little Tiger Press 2016
Cover illustration by Emma Randall
Text and illustrations copyright © Little Tiger Press 2016

Printed in China
ISBN 978-1-84869-416-3
LTP/2700/1967/0917
2 4 6 8 10 9 7 5 3